A Red Fox Book: 0 09 943917 4

First published in Great Britain by The Bodley Head,
an imprint of Random House Children's Books

The Bodley Head edition published 1999
Red Fox edition published 2002

1 3 5 7 9 10 8 6 4 2

Red Fox Books are published by Random House Children's Books,
61-63 Uxbridge Road, London W5 5SA,
a division of The Random House Group, Ltd,
in Australia by Random House Australia (Pty) Ltd,
20 Alfred Street, Milsons Point, Sydney, NSW 2061, Australia,
in New Zealand by Random House New Zealand Ltd,
18 Poland Road, Glenfield, Auckland 10, New Zealand,
and in South Africa by Random House (Pty) Ltd,
Endulini, 5A Jubilee Road, Parktown 2193, South Africa

THE RANDOM HOUSE GROUP Limited Reg. No. 954009
www.randomhouse.co.uk

A CIP catalogue record for this book is available from the British Library.

Printed in Singapore

The Bear Went Over the Mountain

JOHN PRATER

RED FOX

The bear went

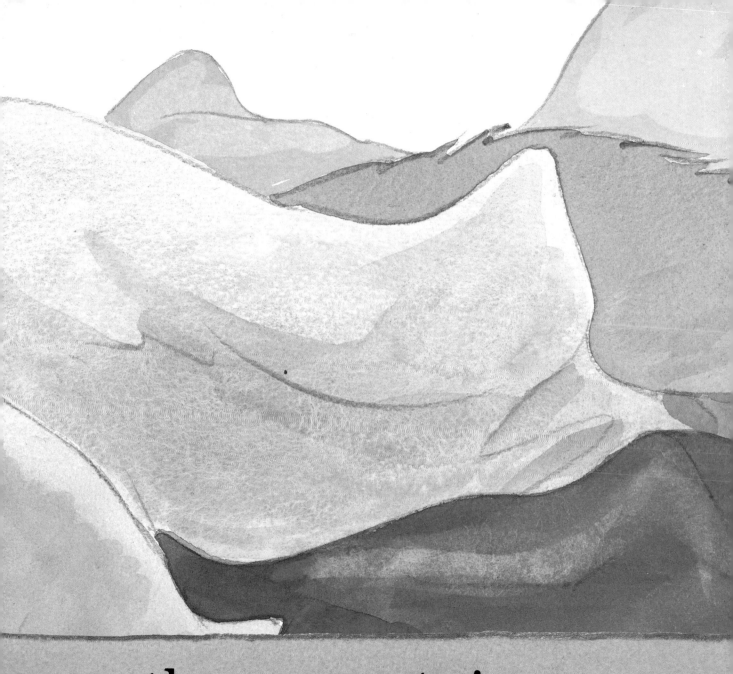

over the mountain...

The bear went

over the mountain...

The bear went

over the mountain...

To see what

he could see.

And the other side

of the mountain...

The other side

of the mountain...

The other side

of the mountain...

Was all that

he could see.

So he went back

over the mountain...

He went back

over the mountain...

He went back

over the mountain...

So very

happily.

Other Baby Bear books to collect: